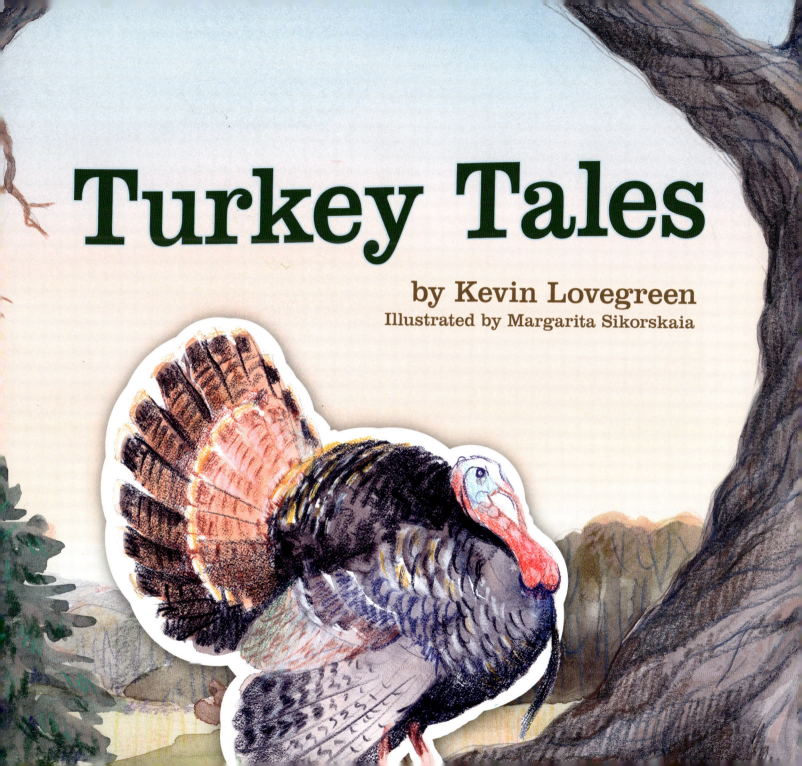

TURKEY TALES © copyright 2012
by Kevin Lovegreen. All rights reserved. No part of this book may be reproduced in any form whatsoever, by photography or xerography or by any other means, by broadcast or transmission, by translation into any kind of language, nor by recording electronically or otherwise, without permission in writing from the author, except by a reviewer, who may quote brief passages in critical articles or reviews.

Illustrated by Maragarita Sikorskaia.

ISBN 13: 978-0-9857179-1-9

Printed in the United States of America

Cover and interior design by James Monroe Design, LLC.

Lucky Luke, LLC.
4335 Matthew Court
Eagan, Minnesota 55123

www.KevinLovegreen.com
Quantity discounts available!

This book is dedicated to Luke and Crystal, my wonderful children.
The time we spend together in the outdoors will always be
dear to my heart. Thank you for the memories.

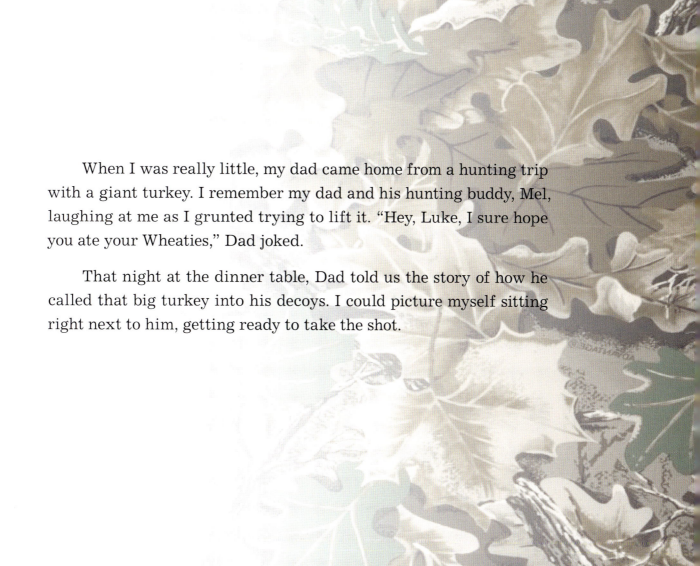

When I was really little, my dad came home from a hunting trip with a giant turkey. I remember my dad and his hunting buddy, Mel, laughing at me as I grunted trying to lift it. "Hey, Luke, I sure hope you ate your Wheaties," Dad joked.

That night at the dinner table, Dad told us the story of how he called that big turkey into his decoys. I could picture myself sitting right next to him, getting ready to take the shot.

The dream of going turkey hunting with Dad finally came true the spring when I was ten. I excitedly helped him pack for the hunt. We both gave Mom a big hug and jumped in our big silver truck. Off we went, heading down the highway. I had a million questions about turkey hunting, but luckily for me, Dad had all the answers.

After a long drive and lots of turkey-hunting talk, we turned off the blacktop and drove down a long dirt driveway. We had the windows down, so Dad's red hair was a little messy as he slid on his baseball cap. I smiled because we were wearing matching lucky hats, each with a turkey on the front. We pulled up to a farm, and there was old, rusted farm equipment everywhere I looked.

We walked over to the barn, where we heard some steel clanging. There was the farmer, all covered in grease and working on a huge tractor. When he saw us, he pulled out a rag from his back pocket and cleaned off his hands as he walked over. He shook Dad's hand first, then mine. I couldn't believe how rough, strong, and giant his hand was.

"Nice to meet you," I said with a smile. "This is my first turkey hunt. I can't wait to get out there and get one."

"There are plenty of birds around. It's up to you to find them. You can head around back. The old trailer house, where you'll be sleeping, is ready," the farmer said.

As our truck came up to the trailer house, Dad suddenly stopped. "Look at that!"

I looked out the window, and there were ten wild turkeys standing in the field just past the trailer!

"See how the toms are all fanned out? That's their way of showing off to the girl turkeys," Dad explained.

"Cool! They are huge!" I said.

After watching for a while, we eased closer to the trailer. The turkeys finally saw the truck, and it was like someone blew an alarm. They all put their heads down and ran up the hill into the woods. I couldn't believe how fast they could move!

We unpacked our gear and laid out our hunting clothes so we would be ready for the early morning. After dinner, we headed to the little back bedroom. I climbed into the top bunk, where my favorite sleeping bag was waiting. It took me a long time to fall asleep because I was thinking about all the turkeys we had seen. By the sound of Dad's snoring, he didn't have any trouble.

I must have finally dozed off because the sound of the alarm clock startled me.

"It's turkey time! You ready?" Dad asked.

"You betcha!" I said through a yawn.

We crawled out of our sleeping bags and put on our hunting clothes. After a quick breakfast, we threw on our boots and went out the door.

Outside, the moon was bright in the sky and there were a million stars. With our shotguns slung over our shoulders, we marched across a cut cornfield to a trail that sliced through the woods.

After we had been walking for a while, Dad stopped and whispered in my ear. "We are going to set up here. Go sit next to that tree, and I will put out the decoys. Be very quiet. The turkeys could be close."

After placing the two decoys in a little opening, he snuck back to me and sat down. Then Dad took my gun and slid two shells in. "The safety is on. You're ready to go," Dad said quietly as he handed it back to me.

He then loaded his gun and laid it down next to him. We pulled on our face masks, and Dad gave me thumbs-up.

Dad made a few quiet calls. We didn't hear a response. Dad's call was supposed to sound like a hen (the girl turkey). In the spring, when the toms hear the hen call, they usually gobble at it, especially when they are waking up, perched high on a big tree branch.

We sat quietly for a few minutes, and then at the far end of the valley, a turkey gobbled. That started a chain reaction. I could hear the gobbles getting closer and closer until two gobbled right behind us. I couldn't believe it! Those gobbles were one of the coolest sounds I had ever heard, kind of like a person yelling as they shook their loose cheeks.

Dad's eyes lit up, and I could tell he was smiling under his mask. "They're right behind us," Dad whispered with excitement. Dad made a couple more hen sounds, and the toms behind us gobbled instantly. Dad's eyes lit up again. I think he was proud he had made them gobble.

Suddenly, a calling crow flew over us, which made every turkey in the woods gobble. It seemed like they were yelling at the crow to get out of *their* woods! As the sun peeked over the trees at the end of the valley, the turkeys gobbled with more intensity. Then we heard some hens yelping behind us. That really got the toms going crazy!

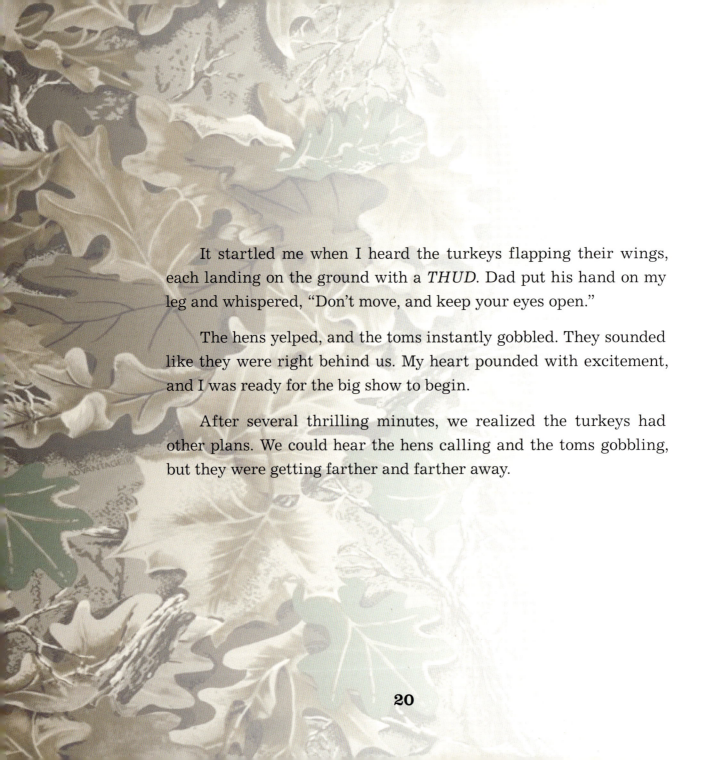

It startled me when I heard the turkeys flapping their wings, each landing on the ground with a *THUD*. Dad put his hand on my leg and whispered, "Don't move, and keep your eyes open."

The hens yelped, and the toms instantly gobbled. They sounded like they were right behind us. My heart pounded with excitement, and I was ready for the big show to begin.

After several thrilling minutes, we realized the turkeys had other plans. We could hear the hens calling and the toms gobbling, but they were getting farther and farther away.

21

Dad shook his head. "The hens took our toms away. It happens all the time. Wow, was that amazing, or what?"

"That was so cool! I thought I was going to get one of those gobblers," I said.

"I did too. But hearing them and getting that close is half the fun. We will sit here a little longer and see if they come back," Dad said.

We didn't have any more action, so we picked up the decoys and headed farther down the trail. As we eased along, we heard a turkey gobble. We both froze in our tracks.

"It sounds like it's coming from the old logging road up ahead. Let's get up there and check it out!" Dad whispered eagerly.

As we hurried down the trail, two or three turkeys started gobbling. We slowed down as we approached the old road.

"Wait here, and I will take a look," Dad said, a little out of breath.

He handed me his gun, got on his hands and knees, and crawled to the edge of the opening. He quickly pulled back and gave me thumbs-up! In a hurry, he pulled one hen decoy out of his vest and eased it out into the trail as far as he could without revealing his body. As soon as the decoy was set, the turkeys began to gobble with more excitement. "They're coming! We need to get ready," Dad said with excitement.

My heart was pounding again as we scurried back into the woods. From the moment Dad put out the decoy, the turkeys didn't stop gobbling. I tried to take a deep breath to calm down, and as I did, my eyes just about popped out of my head. I finally saw my first turkey live in the woods, and it was coming right down the trail.

As I watched in amazement, another turkey appeared behind the first one. I couldn't believe it—two turkeys! I could tell by their small beards they were jakes (young toms). And then I heard the most amazing gobble of all come from behind the second turkey. It was so loud it shook my whole body.

Suddenly, the jakes turned and looked right at me. "Hold your gun steady. They see the barrel shaking," Dad whispered out of the corner of his mouth. They started to get really nervous, and their heads were popping around like they were on springs. "The big one is behind the first two. Let them go by. See if you can take the big one." I just nodded. I'm not sure I could have spoken if I tried.

I balanced my gun on my knee to keep it from shaking. The turkeys knew something wasn't right with me and Dad, but they really wanted to go past us and check out the decoy. At that moment I caught a glimpse of the big tom. I could see his right eye peeking through the brush, trying to see what was causing the jakes to be so nervous. Then the first two started to cluck, the turkeys' warning sound.

Then I could hardly hear Dad say, "Get ready. There he is." Then it happened. Just as the two jakes were turning to leave, the big tom poked his head around the bush and appeared.

"Take him, take him!" Dad urged.

In one motion, I clicked the safety off and raised my gun, aiming at the turkey's head. I pulled the trigger. *BANG!* The gun rang out.

"You got him, you got him!" Dad yelped.

We both jumped up and ran to him. The giant tom was lying on his back, and his feet were sticking up in the air.

"You did it, buddy! It was a perfect shot!" Dad said as he high-fived me.

"YES! Whoo-hoo!" I yelled

"Look how big he is!" Dad said in amazement.

"He's a giant!" I beamed.

"All your practice shooting paid off. I'm so proud of you, Luke. You're a great hunter."

"Thanks, Dad," I said with a beaming smile.

Dad and I took a lot of pictures and kept telling the story over and over to each other.

I couldn't wait to tell Mom the good news, so I called her up as soon as we got back. I told her every detail, and I could tell by her voice she was really excited for me. "You and Dad sure make a good team. I'm proud of you, buddy, and I'm glad you're having such a good time!" Mom said.

After talking to Mom, we weighed and measured the turkey. He was twenty-five pounds, had one-and-a-half-inch spurs on his legs, and had a thirteen-inch beard. He was a true trophy.

We hopped in the truck and drove around to the farmhouse, where we found the farmer doing some chores. I jumped out and ran to the back of the truck.

"Check out this beauty!" I said proudly to the farmer.

He looked in and grinned so wide his eyes seemed to squint.

"That's one nice turkey, young man. Your dad told me that you were lucky, and he wasn't kidding."

"I sure am. Thank you very much for allowing us to hunt on your farm. This place is amazing!"

"Well, I'm glad you had fun and that you got yourself such a nice bird. Now you have to help your dad get *his* turkey," he said with a wink.

Later that night, snuggled in my sleeping bag, many thoughts floated through my mind.

I smiled, picturing my whole family sitting around the Thanksgiving dinner table, watching Dad carving MY turkey for everyone to eat.

My smile grew as my thoughts shifted back to the hunt. I realized that my dream came true. I WAS sitting next to Dad when the turkey came in, and I was lucky enough to get the shot.

Drifting off to sleep, I began dreaming about other hunting adventures . . . when would they come true?

Lucky Luke's 25 lb. turkey

About the Author

Kevin Lovegreen was born and raised in Minnesota, where he lives with his loving wife and two amazing children. Hunting, fishing, and the outdoors have always been a big part of his life. From chasing squirrels as a child to chasing elk as an adult, Kevin loves the thrill of hunting, but even more, he loves telling stories of the adventure. Presenting at schools and connecting with kids about the outdoors is one of his favorite things to do.

Other Books in the Series

To order books or learn about school visits please go to:
www.KevinLovegreen.com